ISBN 978-0-259-50681-2
PIBN 10269646

JACQUES BALMAT,

OR

The First Ascent of Mont Blanc.

A TRUE STORY.

BY

T. LOUIS OXLEY.

LONDON:
KERBY AND ENDEAN, 190 OXFORD STREET.
OATLANDS PARK: J. NORTH.
AND ALL BOOKSELLERS.
1881.

TO

F. J. CAMPBELL, Esq.

Principal of the Royal Normal College for the Blind,

THE FIRST BLIND TRAVELLER

WHO ASCENDED MONT BLANC,

THIS STORY IS DEDICATED.

T. L. O.

PREFACE.

Whilst passing a month, during the last summer at Chamounix, I met with M. Payot's "Guide Itineraire au Mont Blanc," in which I found the following story. It was taken by him from Alexandre Dumas' book of Travel in Switzerland.

In addition to Jacques Balmat's vive voce narrative, I have given Michael Carrier's account of the sad death of the intrepid Climber.

This story will be as a thrice-told-tale to the Alpinist.

Still there are mauy who have not seen Mont Blanc, and many who have never heard the name of the man who first ascended to the summit of the highest mountain in Europe.

Oatlands Park,

March, 1881.

PREFACE.

JACQUES BALMAT was born in the village of Pèlerins, in the commune of Chamonix, in the year 1762. His fore-fathers had long been peasant proprietors, but his tastes differed from theirs; he was endowed with a vivid imagination and with invincible courage, and in order to increase the latter gift he constantly explored the surrounding mountains in search of minerals, for the science of which he had a perfect passion. His audacious courage had made him renowned even amongst his dauntless companions, and his ambition made him thirst to signalize himself by some memorable exploit. He therefore determined to gain the award which De Saussure had promised to the first man who should discover a path by which the summit of Mont Blanc could be reached. Numerous attempts had been made to attain this object, but hitherto without result.

Let us leave Jacques Balmat to relate his intrepid adventures in his own way, and with his quaint and naive preface to them.

"The determination to reach the summit of Mont Blanc was jogging in my brain night and day. During the day I used to ascend the Brevent, where I passed hours in trying to see a way to my coveted summit. I felt that I should live in a sort of purgatory if I did not succeed, and I could not resist this impulse to go to the Brevent. At night I had hardly closed my eyes when I dreamt that I was on my climb of discovery." . . . .

We will give but the last of his numerous dreams—it is too characteristic and too delicious to omit. In it he says: "I fixed my nails into the rock that they might act like cramps—I felt I was going to fall—I said to myself: 'Jacques Balmat my friend, if thou dost not catch hold of that branch above thy head, thine account will soon be settled.' "—The accursed branch could only be touched with the tips of my fingers—I raised myself up by my knees like a chimne sweep. Ah that branch! now I clutched at it! I shall never forget that night! my wife awoke me with a great slap . . . imagine! . . . I was sticking fast to her ear all the time, and drawing it out as if it had been a piece of indian rubber! after such an affair as this I said: Jacques Balmat you must now get the right sort of heart in earnest! I thereupon got out of bed and put on my gaiters. 'Where art thou going?' said my wife. 'In search of crystals,' I replied.—I would not tell her what 1 was going to do. 'Do not thou be anxious if thou dost not see me this evening; if I have not retnrned by nine o'clock I shall sleep on the mountain.'

I took a strong stock with good iron points double the length and thickness of an ordinary one. I filled a gourd with eau-de-vie. I put a morsel of bread in my pocket, and away I started.

I had repeatedly tried to ascend by the "Mer

de glace:" but the *Mont Maudit* had always barred my way. Then I used to return by the *Aiguille du Goûté;* but to ascend from there to the '*Dôme du Goûté* there is an 'arète' (a backbone of rock) a quarter of a league long, and from one to two feet wide, and below a depth of 1800 feet! This time I was resolved to try another route. I began by the one which leads to the mountain of the '*Côte;*' after three hours ascent, I reached the glacier des Bossons: I crossed it—it was not difficult to do so; four hours later I was at the Grands Mulets—that was something. I had earned my breakfast.—I ate a crust and drank off a cup. So far so good: but one had not then mounted so often to the Grands Mulets as to find a plateau—one was not quite at one's case there, I can assure you. At the end of two hours and a half of research I found a place bare of snow for about six or seven feet—it was here I determined to await the coming day—it was then about 7 o'clock. It was better to stay there than on the snow. I broke off my second crust and drank my second draught; then I installed myself on the rock where I was going to pass the night. It did not take me long to make my bed. Towards nine o'clock I saw a shadow rise from the valley like a thick smoke; it advanced slowly towards me. At half past nine it reached and enveloped me. Notwithstanding this shroud, I could see above me the last reflected rays of the setting sun which seemed loath to leave the highest point of Mont Blanc. But they did disappear—and with them the day. Turned as I was towards Chamonix; I had, on my left side the immense plain of snow which reaches to the Dôme du Goûté, and on my right—within reach of my hand—a precipice 800 feet deep: I dared not go to sleep for fear of falling outside my bed whilst dreaming. I sat on my bag and stamped my feet and clapped my hands incessantly to keep up the circulation. Soon the moon rose; pale, veiled in a circle of clouds: at eleven I saw a nasty mist cloud coming from the Aiguille de Gôuté, which as soon as it reached me smacked me in the face with a dash of snow:—when I had covered my face with my handkerchief I said 'Good! get along with you!' Every moment I heard the fall of avalanches which rolled down with a horrible rumbling sound like thunder. The glaciers cracked, and with every crack the mountain shook under me. Neither hungry nor thirsty was I, but I experienced a singular kind of headache, the pain beginning at the crown of the head and reaching to the eye-brows. The mist-fog continued; my breath became congealed on my handkerchief; the snow having penetrated through my clothes, I felt as if I were naked. I redoubled my movements and compelled myself to sing in order to drive away a heap of horrible ideas which began to haunt my mind. But my voice was lost in the snow: no echo answered to it: all was death-like in the midst of this frozen nature: and thus my voice had a strange effect upon me: I became afraid that I should commit suicide.

At last, at two o'clock, the sky began to whiten towards the east; I felt my courage returning as the sun arose and struggled with the clouds which shrouded Mont Blanc. I trusted that he would chase them away, but at four o'clock they became more dense; the effects of the sun becoming feebler, I came to the conclusion that it would be impossible to ascend further that day; but in order not to waste such an opportunity, I explored the neighbouring glaciers and passed the whole day in reconnoitering the best passages. As evening advanced and the mists followed, I descended to the *Bec-à-l'oiseau,* where night overtook me. I passed this one better than the last as I was not upon the ice and could sleep a little:—I awoke frozen through and through:—and it was only at the village of Moud that my clothes began to thaw.

I had gone about a hundred steps past the last houses in this village when I met François Paccard, Joseph Carrier, and Jean Michel Fournier—three guides—they had their bags and batons, and wore their climbing costume. I asked them where they were bound for—they replied that they were in search of some goats which they had given to the care of some shepherds—but, as these animals were not worth more than four francs each, this answer made me think that they wished to deceive me. I felt convinced that they were going to attempt the ascent, in which I had failed, and consequently to obtain the reward which De Saussure had promised to the first who should reach the summit of Mont Blanc. One or two questions which Piccard put to me about different points, and whether one could sleep at the Bec-à-l'oiseau confirmed me in my opinion. I replied that it was covered with snow, and that as a station it appeared to me un-advisable. I then saw him exchange a sign with the others, which I pretended not to notice; they retired apart and consulted together, and ended by proposing that we should all ascend together:—I accepted—but having promised my wife that I would not stay away more than three days, and not wising to break my promise, I went home to tell her not to be uneasy, to change my stockings and gaiters, and to get some provisions.

At eleven o'clock at night I started again,

without having been in bed; and at one o'clock I rejoined my comrades at the Bec-à-l'oiseau, four leagues below where I had slept the evening before. They were sleeping like marmots. I awoke them—in an instant they were all on their feet, and we all four set forward on our journey. This day we crossed the glacier of Tacconnay, and ascended as far as the Grands Mulets, where two nights before I had passed such hideous hours; then taking a course to the right, about three o'clock we reached the Dôme du Goûté. Already one of us, Piccard, was short of wind; a little above the Grands Mulets he had lain down, covered with the coat of one of his comrades. Arriving at last at the top of the Dôme we saw something black moving on the Aiguille du Goûté; we could not distinguish what it was; we could not tell whether it were a man or a chamois. We shouted out, and something answered us;—we remained silent awaiting a second cry; when these words reached us: "Ohé! Halt! there are others who wish to ascend with you." We halted; and whilst waiting, Piccard, who had regained his wind, arrived.

At the end of half an hour the new comers joined us; they were Pierre Balmat and Marie Coultet, who had made a bet with others that they would reach the Dôme due Goûté before us. They had lost their bet. During this time, to utilize every moment, I went on a voyage of discovery. I *clomb* towards the Arête, now called the Bosse du Dromadaire, and got a quarter of a league nearer to the animal, on the aforesaid Arête.

Soon after I had quitted the others they had tried the same path, and had come to the conclusion that they were attempting the impossible. It was a rope-dancer's path—but that was all the same to me. I believe that I should have succeeded in reaching the end of it if it had not been cut in two with *crevasses;* besides the Arête was so sharp one could not walk upon it, so not wishing to have to return backwards and astride, I retraced my way to the place where I had left my comrades. I however found nothing but my bag—they had all gone!! At the sight of such temerity, and seeing that nothing would deter me, they left me, and quickly took the path with their backs towards Chamonix, supposing that I, being agile would soon catch them up. I found myself then alone, and for an instant I was as it were suspended between the wish to join them and the desire to attempt the ascent by myself. Their desertion had piqued me; something told me that I should succeed this time. I took up my bag and once more set off. It was now four in the afternoon. I crossed the Grand Plateau as far as the glacier of Brevna, from whence I could see *Courmayeur* and the valley *D'Aosti* in Piedmont. The mist was on the summit of Mont Blanc. I did not attempt to ascend, less from a fear that I should lose myself, than from a feeling of certainty that the others *not seeing* me on the summit would never believe that I had reached it. I took advantage of what remained of the day to seek a a shelter, and spent an hour in vain in so doing; and, as I recollected that awful night—you know—I resolved to return home. I commenced my descent, but when I arrived at the Grand Plateau, not having provided myself with spectacles nor a green veil, the snow had so fatigued my eyes that I could see nothing. I had a kind of dazzling giddiness, which caused me to see great drops of blood. I sat down in order to restore myself; I let my head fall between my hands; at the end of half an hour my sight had come back, but the night had come with it; I had no time to lose. I arose to go, but had scarcely taken a hundred steps when I felt by my bâton that there was no depth of ice under my feet. I was at the edge of the great crevasse in which three guides had been lost. "Ah!" I said to it, "I know thee." In fact in the morning we had crossed it by a bridge of ice covered with snow—this I tried to find; but the night was growing darker and darker, and my sight worse and worse.—I could not find it. The pain in my head, of whieh I have spoken, again attacked me; I felt no desire to eat or drink; violent palpitations of the heart made me almost vomit. I must make up my mind to remain close to the crevasse until day break: to find the bridge of ice would take me another hour. I put down my bag on the snow; I made a curtain of my handkerchief, and did my best to prepare for such a night as before. Being 12,000 feet high, I must expect a much more intense cold. A fine needle-like snow froze me; I felt a languor and an irresistable desire to sleep; thoughts the most sad come across my mind, like unto those of death. I knew that these gloomy ideas and this longing for sleep were bad signs, and that if I had the misfortune to close my eyes in sleep, I should never open them again. From the place where I was I could see the lights of Chamonix where my comrades who had deserted me, were warming themselves by their firesides, or were comfortably in in bed. 'Perhaps not one of them' (I said to myself) has given me a thought; or if one of them has thought of Balmat, he says, whilst rousing the embers of his fire, or pulling the coverlet more over his ears: 'At this moment that imbecile of a Balmat is amusing himself by beating the soles of his boots together!' 'Keep up your courage, Balmat!' It was not that I wanted courage now, but strength;—man is not made of iron—and I felt that I was ill. In the short intervals of silence between the momentary falls of avalanches and the cracking of the glacier, I heard the barking of a dog in the village of Courmayeur, although the village was a league and a half from where I was. This noise took my thoughts away from myself; it was the only sound from the world below which reached me. Towards midnight the dog ceased to bark, and I fell back into that terrible silence which was like unto that of churchyard:—for I took no account of the noise of the avalanches and of the glaciers, whose sounds frightened me. About two o'clock I saw the same white line, of which I have already spoken, dawn on the horizon; the sun followed it as before, and Mont Blanc had also put on his wig; and when he does that, he is in a bad humour and one must not provoke him. I know his character, and I think it right to let other know it too. As we say in the valley: "When he smokes his pipe, one must not try to put it out." At last when daybreak came, I was frozen; but by dint of friction, and practising the most absurd gymnastics, my limbs became more supple, and I was able to begin exploring once more. I had observed, when descending to the Grand Plateau, that half-way down there was an incline,—steep it is true—but every where accessible, and leading straight to the top of the *Rochers Rouges*, I decided to scale it; but found it so steep and the snow so hard that I could only hold on by making holes with the iron point of my stock; I succeeded in clinging to it, but I felt extreme fatigue and weariness. It was not an amusing thing to be suspended by one leg—so to speak—with an abyss under one; and to be obliged to cut the ice with the already blunted point of an Alpen stock. At length by force of patience and perseverance I gained les Rochers Rouges. Oh! said I, "*from this spot to the summit there's nothing more to hinder you; all is joined together like one piece of ice!!*" But I was again frozen through and through, and almost dead with hunger and thirst; it was late;—I *must* descend—but this time with a *certainty* of succeeding during the first spell of propitious weather.

When I reached home I was almost blind. When my sight became somewhat restored I went (in order to avoid the flies) to lie down in the grange—and there I slept for 48 hours without waking.

Three weeks elapsed without bringing any favorable change in the weather, and without diminishing my ardour to make a third attempt. I imparted the secret of my discovery to Dr. Paccard, and associated him with my future intentions. It was agreed that we should start together the first fine day.

At last on the 8th of August, 1786, the weather appeared sufficiently settled to hazard another trial. I went to Paccard and said to him "Now Doctor, are you up to it? Have you any fear of snow; of ice; of precipices? Speak out like a man." "I have fear of naught when I am with thee, Balmat!" replied Paccard. "Well then," I said, "the moment has come to creep upon la Taupinière."

The Doctor said he was quite ready, but when he was about to shut his door, I think his courage began to fail him a little, for the key would not leave the lock—he turned it first one way and then another. "Stay, Balmat" said he, "we should do well to take two guides with us." "No," I replied, "I ascend with you alone, or you ascend with others. I wish to be the first, not the second." He reflected for a moment, then drew out the key, put it into his pocket, and followed me mechanically with bent head. In another instant he pricked up his ears.—"Ah well! I have confidence in thee, Balmat. Go on! For the rest, God's mercy!" Then he began to sing, but not quite in tune. This seemed to worry the Doctor. Whereupon I took his arm, and said, "This is not all Doctor; no one must know of our project except our wives." A third person was however obliged to be taken into our confidence: the shop-keeper of whom we bought the syrup to mix with our eau-de-vie, which, unmixed would have been too strong for such an undertaking as ours. As this woman was incredulous about what we told her, we invited her to look the next morning at nine o'clock, towards the side of the *Dôme du Goûté*. All our little matters being settled, we bade adieu to our wives and departed about five in the afternoon, one taking one side of the Arve, and the other the other, so that no one might suspect where we were going, and we met again at the village of la Côtè or du Mont. I had brought a coverlet, which served to enwrap the Doctor as they swathe an infant. Thanks to this precaution he passed a good night; as for me, I slept without waking until half past one. At two the white line appeared; and soon the sun arose without a cloud, without a mist, beautiful and brilliant, promising us a famous journey at last. In a quarter of an hour's time we were engaged with the glacier of Taconnaz. which we crossed without any accident, and soon we left the Grands Mulets below us. I showed the Doctor where I had spent the night: he made a significant grimace, and kept silence for some minutes—then stopping all at once. "Dost thou think Balmat that we shall arrive to-day at the top of Mont Blanc?" I saw well what he was coming to—but I reassured him laughingly, without promising him anything. We went on for two hours and reached the Grand Plateau. The wind overtook us and became stronger and stronger. At length, after having scaled that well-remembered vertical barrier, we reached the rock of the Petits-Mulets. Here a gust of wind carried away the Doctor's hat, although it was tied on. Hearing his exclamation I turned round, and beheld his comfortable cap bounding down towards Courmayeur. He looked as if he were going after it with outstretched arms. "Oh!" said I, "we shall never see it again! it has gone into Piedmont; Bon voyage!" It seemed as if the wind took offence at this pleasantry, for scarcely had I shut my mouth when there came so violent a blast that we were obliged to lie flat on our faces in order not to follow the hat. We were not able to get up for ten minutes; the wind thrashed the mountains and passed whistling over our heads The Doctor was discouraged;—I only thought of the shop-keeper, who ought to be looking out for us at that moment to see if we were on the Dôme du Goûté. At the first respite which the 'bise' gave us, I got up; but the Doctor would only consent to follow on his hands and knees. In this way we pursued the course of a small mountain until we could see from it the village of Chamonix. Having gained this point, with my glasses I made out, 12,000 feet below us in the valley, our commercial friend with about fifty others, looking at us through their telescopes. A consideration for his amour propre made the Doctor get upon his legs;—the moment he stood up we saw that we were recognized—he, by his great coat, I by my usual clothes. The people in the valley saluted us with their hats; I replied with mine;—that of the Doctor was absent on an indefinite holiday. Paccard had spent all his energy in rising to his feet, and neither by the enconragements which he received from below, not by those which I gave him, could he be induced to continue the ascent. After exhausting all my eloquence, and seeing I should only lose time, I told him to keep himself as warm as he could, and not to stand still. He listened without understanding me, and replied: "yes—yes" in order to get rid of me. I knew he must suffer from the cold; I myself was almost paralysed; I left him the bottle, and started off alone, telling him that I would come and fetch him. "Yes—yes" he replied. I urged him again not to stand still, and off I went. I had not gone thirty paces when I returned, and found him, instead of moving about and stamping with his feet, sitting down, with his back to the glacial wind. This was at all events some precaution.

From this moment there was no great difficulty to encounter; but the higher I mounted the less respirable became the air: every ten steps I was obliged to stop like an asthmatic man; it seemed as if I had no lungs, and that my chest was empty. I tied my handkechief round my mouth and breathed through it, and this relieved me a little.

The cold had become almost insupportable: it took me an hour to walk a quarter of a league. Still I went on, with head bent down, until, all at once, coming to a point which I did not recognizet I lifted my head, and, lo! and behold!—*at las*, I had conquered Mont Blanc!

Then I cast my eyes around me—trembling lest I had deceived myself and I should find some aiguille, some new point which I had not the power to ascend; for the joints of my legs seemed to be kept in their places only by the aid of my trousers. No—I was at the end of so many explorings, so many unfruitful researches. I had reached the goal where no one had as yet been, not even the eagle nor the chamois; alone, I was here, without other aid than my will and my strength; all that surrounded me seemed to belong to me. It was four o'clock when I contemplated this giddy panorama; I looked down on Chamonix, I waved my hat, I saw through my glass that they replied by doing the same. All the village was on the "Place."

The first moment of exultation over, I thought of

my poor Doctor. I descended as quickly as possible, calling out his name, and was terrified by not hearing him answer me; at the end of a quarter of an hour I saw him in the distance, round as a ball, but making no movement in spite of my shouts, which certainly must have reached him. I found him with his head between his knees, crouched like a cat when it makes itself into a muff. I took him by the shoulder; he raised his head mechanically. I told him that I had reached the summit of Mont Blanc; this news seemed to interest him in the most mediocre way, for in reply he asked where he could go to bed and to sleep. I rejoined that he had come to ascend Mont Blanc, and ascend it he should. I raised him up; I took him by the shoulders and made him walk some steps; he was as if drunk, and it appeared all the same to him whether he went to the one side or the other, up hill, or down hill. However, the exercise which I made him take restored his circulation a little, and he asked me if I had accidentally put into my pocket the hare-skin gloves which I had made expressly for my ascents, and which we call here "mitaine" being without separation between the fingers. Situated as I then was, I would have refused them *both* to my own brother;—I gave him one of them.

At six o'clock I was once more on the summit of Mont Blanc, and my worthy Doctor too. Although the sun still shed bright rays of light, the sky was of a deep dark blue, and I conld see the stars shining. Below us were ice, snow, rocks, pines; a panorama impossible to describe. I tried to make my Doctor a partaker of the extacy into which the spectable which unfolded itself before our eyes had plunged me:—it was in vain; he saw nothing; the state in which he was had deprived him of his morale, and the effort to make him enjoy such contemplation was labour lost. As for me, I suffered no longer, I was no longer fatigued. I scarcely felt that difficulty of breathing which an hour ago had almost made me abandon my undertaking. In this state of rapture I remained on the summit for thirty minutes. It was seven o'clock—we had but two more hours of daylight—we must descend. I took hold of Paccard, I waved my hat as a last signal, and we began our downward journey. There was no track to direct us; the wind was so cold that even the surface of the snow was not melted; all we found was here and there on the ice the small holes which our stocks had made. Paccard was like a child, without energy or will; I guided him in the good parts, and carried him over the bad. Night began to fall whilst we crossed the crevasse at the foot of the Grand Plateau. It came upon us all at once. At each step Paccard stopped, declaring he would go no further; I made him go on, not by persuasion, which he no longer understood, but by sheer force. At eleven o'clock we left the regions of ice, aud placed our feet on firm ground. It was more than three hours since we had lost all reflection from the sun; this being the case, I permitted Paccard to halt; and when preparing to wrap him again in the coverlet I found that he did not help me as before. On my remarking this to him, "it is for the best of all reasons," said he, "I have no longer any use or feeling in my hands." I drew off his gloves; his hands were as white as those of death. As for myself, the hand on which was the leather glove, in place of the hare-skin one, was in the same condition as his two. I said to him: "out of four hands, three are of no use." This communication did not interest him; all he desired was to go to bed and sleep. But he said, "rub the frozen parts with snow; the remedy is not far to seek." I began the operation with him, and ended it with myself; soon the circulation was restored, and with it the warmth, but with it pain as acute as if each vein were being pricked with needles. I rolled my baby in his swaddling clothes and lay down under the shelter of a rock; we ate a morsel and drank a cup, lay as close to each other as possible, and fell asleep. The next day at six, I was awoke by Paccard who said, "It is droll, Balmat, I can hear the birds chirping and singing, and yet I cannot see the daylight; perhaps I cannot open my eyes; see if they have become like those of "a grand Duke."* I told him that he was mistaken, that he ought to see. He then asked for some snow, which he melted in his hands and mixed with brandy, and applied to his eyelids;—this operation was of no avail, it only made them smart the more. 'Balmat, I am blind!!" "It seems very like it," I replied. "How am I to descend?" "Take hold of the strap of my bag, and walk behind me. That is the way!" By this means we reached the village of Côte.

As I feared that my wife would be anxious, I left the Doctor, who felt his way home by tapping with his stock, and I returned to mine. When I beheld myself! I was not recognizable. I had red eyes, a black face, and blue lips; each time that I yawned or laughed the blood spirted from my lips:—in fact I was a spectre! . . . . .

Four days afterwards I set out for Geneva to announce the news to M. de Saussure—but some Englishmen had already preceded me in this mission.

*A nocturnal bird of prey.

We left Jacques at the moment when he was hastening to Geneva to announce to De Saussure the success of his enterprise.

We next hear of him, after the lapse of several years, in Paris, on a visit to Alexander Dumas pére, with whom he visited the museums, public buildings, etc. of the Capital. Being taken to see a Panorama of Chamounix and Mont Blanc, Balmat was so struck by the reality of the scene, that he burst into tears, and was seized with such intense "Mal-du-pays" that he was obliged to return immediately to his beloved valley.

The cultivation of Balmat's humble patriomony did not satisfy his ambition; — he dreamed of riches; — he many times engaged in commercial enterprises; hating restraint, he rarely undertook the office of guide, preferring hazardous, and more lucrative expeditions in search of minerals.

In September, 1834, giving credence to vague rumours, that there existed a rich vein of gold on the side of one of the high peaks which bound the valley of Sixt to the N. E., Jacques Balmat set out to discover it. He arrived near the spot indicated—to find it inaccessible. It was necessary to traverse a narrow ledge of rock, overhanging a frightful precipice—the sight of the danger daunted him, and for the moment he abandoned the attempt. Sometime afterwards, having obtained the assistance of an intrepid Chamois-hunter, he returned to the charge; and now in spite of the prayers and expostulations of his comrade, persisted—the fascination was too strong for him—he ventured upon the narrow ledge—took several steps:—and—disappeared—The hunter, horrified, in despair, in a state bordering on distraction returned alone. No help could avail the unhappy Balmat; his death must have been instantaneous.

Picture to yourself a fall of more than 400 feet into an abyss covered with masses of rock, over which the avalanches swept continually, and you will have a faint idea of this horrible tomb.

At first the chief details of this melancholy accident were unknown at Chamounix; Balmat's companion hiding the truth, lest suspicion should rest upon him. Some shepherds of Sixt had also seen the unhappy man disappear, but kept silence from various reasons; the discovery of the precious mine being the main one.

The sons of Balmat made several fruitless attempts to recover their father's body. The information thee were able to acquire, respecting the scene of thy accident, was very meagre, and even had they had more reliable intelligence to go upon, they could never have succeeded in raising it out of the profound abyss.

Nineteen years rolled away without anyone thinking of undertaking fresh researches. The frightful description that was given of the abyss, at the bottom of which the unfortunate Balmat was lying, and the dangers that must be encountered, deterred the bravest hearts.

*"In September, 1853, some of our excellent guides, having had occasion to approach the spot whence Balmat had fallen, collected all the particulars they could about the place, and on their

* Michael Carrier's account.

return to the valley of Sixt, where they had to conduct some travellers, they proposed to me (Michael Carrier) and others to make an expedition to discover, if possible, the remains of Balmat, in order to procure for them, Christian burial. The proposition was received with enthusiasm; we set out, to the number of ten, for the valley of Sixt. The whole body of guides would, had it been necessary, have accompanied us, but we thought our party sufficiently numerous and capable; as, in its members, were united, courage, skill, and prudence.

We crossed the Brevent, descended into the valley of Diosaz, climbed the Col d' Anterne, and came down by the châlets of that name to the valley of Sixt.

After consultating two of the best guides of the place, and gaining all the information they could afford us respecting the passes and names of the localities we had to explore, we set off for the valley, from whence the only exit is by steep narrow chamois-tracks. Selecting one of these, about 3 miles and three quarters from the principal village of Sixt, our interprid guides commenced a rapid ascent along the edge of the precipice; first they had to climb grassy slopes, alternating with almost perpendicular rocks, where they were obliged to make use of both hands and feet; then to cross several deep ravines, before arriving at the foot of a glacier surmounted by a wall of rock, from the height of which the eye could penetrate the dreadful abyss, which contained the remains of the first guide who had ever planted his adventurous foot on the top of Mont Blanc.

It was with sentiments of deep emotion that our guides regarded the frightful chasm, where Balmat had met so tragic a fate. Common prudence counselled them only to sound this gulf with their eyes, as, in addition to its horrible depth, every moment, avalanches of stones and ice engulfed themselves.

Auguste Balmat, one of the great nephews of Balmat, well known amongst the guides for his bravery, desired to be let down by a rope, and began the descent by the side, slipping every moment on the rotten schist which broke away under his feet. He had not gone far in this adventurous and daring enterprise, when he gave the signal agreed upon, to be drawn up and was received by his companions, and embraced by them, as they knelt on the last ledge of the precipice, as one does by an open grave. It was in truth an eternal tomb, consecrated by the fatal accident.

After having carefully indentified the places designated by the information collected the day before, and assured ourselves of the impossibility of pursuing more extended researches, we tore ourselves away from this horrible place and returned to Sixt, after having made a long detour, by the Glacier and the Pointe de Roant, as far as the Col-de-Chasse-roue.

The next day, September 22nd, we passed by the Châlets of Sales to return to Chamounix.

However to convince ourselves that nothing

had been neglected, and that the directions given were correct, we had a fresh and confidential interview with the Chamois-hunter who had accompanied Jacques Balmat on his last, and fatal expedition.

I had taken a sketch of the scene, which I put before him, whereupon he immediately recognised the various localities, and pointed out, without hesitation, the spot from whence Jacques Balmat had fallen."

So ends Michael Carrier's account.

* * * * * *

What Michael Carrier had long wished was accomplished August 10th, 1878, when a Monument was erected to the Memory of Jacques Balmat by the French Geograpicial Society, and placed in front of the Parish Church at Chamounix.

Lightning Source UK Ltd.
Milton Keynes UK
UKHW01f2359051018
330081UK00021B/531/P

9 780259 506812